WHAT TRUTH?

Written by Elizabeth Urbanowicz
Illustrated by Miranda Duncan

A Foundation Worldview Book

Get a free companion activity sheet for this book
at FoundationWorldview.com/truth

Published by Foundation Worldview
PO Box 915
Evans, GA 30809

FoundationWorldview.com

Hello There!

My name's Sebastian and this is my friend Gregg. I am so excited that you are with us today! We are about to go on a thinking journey.

When you turn the page, you will see
a word written in BIG LETTERS.

What word did you just see?

That's right!

TRUTH

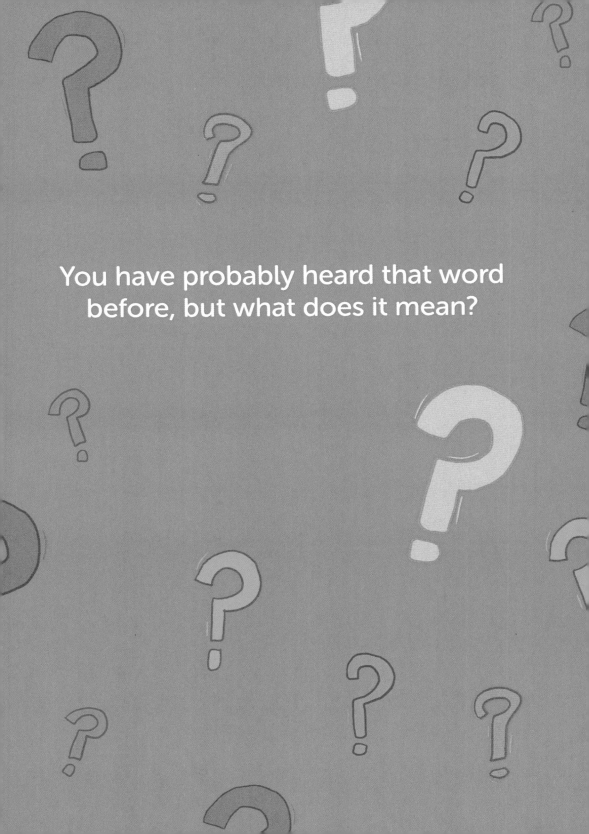

You have probably heard that word before, but what does it mean?

Let's pretend your mom found her favorite lamp broken on the floor. She would probably ask you to tell her the TRUTH about what happened.

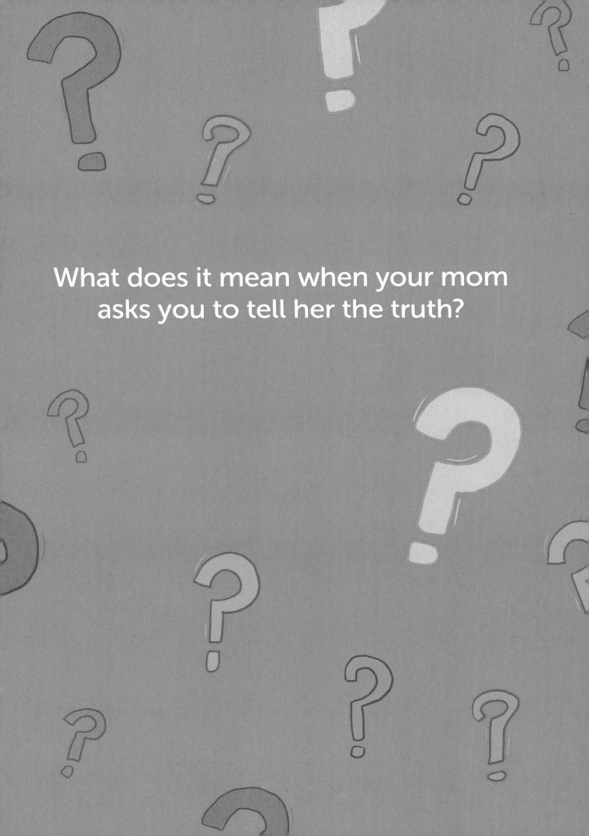

What does it mean when your mom asks you to tell her the truth?

It means she wants you to tell her what REALLY happened.

That's because truth is what is real!
Say that with me!

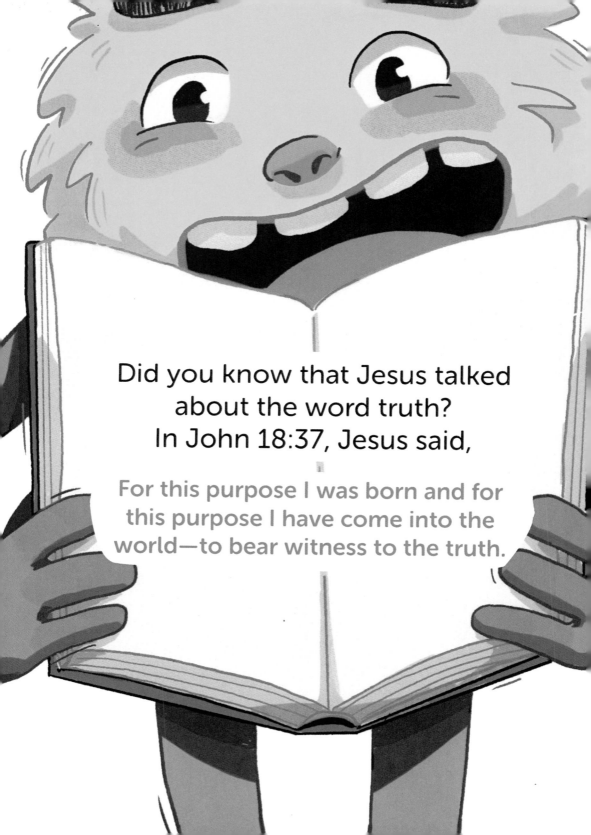

Did you know that Jesus talked about the word truth?
In John 18:37, Jesus said,

For this purpose I was born and for this purpose I have come into the world—to bear witness to the truth.

If Jesus came to tell people about the truth, truth must be pretty important to God.

That is why it is important for us to figure out what is TRUE and what is NOT TRUE.

Let's practice finding truth together.
If I say a sentence that is true, spread
out your arms and say,

If I say a sentence that is not true, cross your arms like an X and say,

Are you ready?

Grass is usually green.

Is this true?

Yes, the grass is usually green.
So that is ...

Are you ready for another one?

Puppies fly in the air.

Is this true?

No, that is silly. Puppies do not fly
in the air.

So that is...

Here comes the next one!

Elephants are the same size as my finger.

No, elephants are huge and our fingers are small.

So that is...

Okay, here's another one.

Water is wet.

Is that

TRUE?

Yes, water is wet.

So that is...

Here's another one...

Snow is very hot.

Is that TRUE?

No, snow is very cold, not hot.

So that is...

Are you ready for one more?

The Bible tells us God is the Creator.

Is this true?

Yes, the Bible does tell us that God is the Creator. So that is...

You did a great job
with that game!

Now let's think back to the word truth.

Do you remember what

TRUTH

is?

TRUTH is what is REAL!
Say that with me!

And now the truth is,
this book has come to an end.

Made in the USA
Monee, IL
14 December 2024

73942638R00029